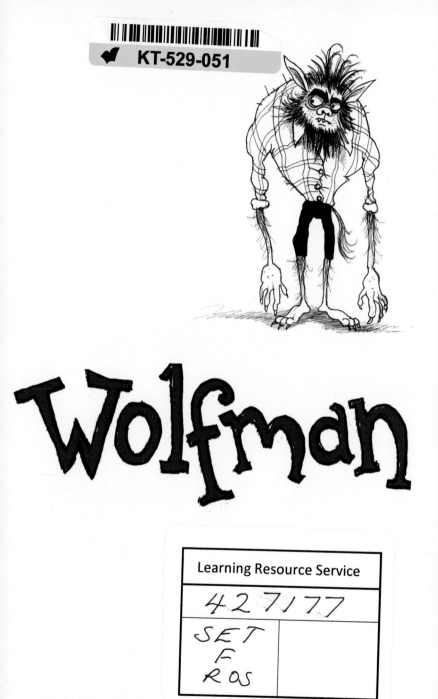

Wolfman

Published in 2013 in Great Britain by
Barrington Stoke Ltd
18 Walker Street, Edinburgh, EH3 7LP

www.barringtonstoke.co.uk

This story was first published in a different form in
Read Me a Story, Please, Orion Children's Books, 1998

Individual ISBN 978-1-78112-302-7
Pack ISBN 978-1-78112-308-9

Not available separately

Printed in China by Leo

www.barringtonstoke.co.uk

MICHAEL ROSEN

Illustrated by Chris Mould

Wolfman

People were running down the street
screaming.

"Look out! Look out! Wolfman has escaped!"

The people were right.

Beware of Wolfman

Wolfman had broken out of his cage and now he was roaring and rampaging around town.

Everyone was rushing to get indoors.

They were very afraid.

Outside, Wolfman was ripping up paving stones. He was biting into trees and eating lamp-posts.

It was the most horrible thing ever.

The Prime Minister said, "Send in the army!"

But the army sent back a message. It said,
"Sorry, we can't come. We're too scared."

Things looked bad.

Wolfman was heading down Coppers Road.
People were looking out from behind their
curtains.

'Please, please, please don't come near our house, Wolfman,' they were thinking.

But Wolfman marched on.

Where was Wolfman going?

To the park?

No.

To the swimming pool?

No.

The people saw that Wolfman was heading for the house where the Chief of Police lived. And the Chief of Police was in the back room, hiding behind the armchair.

Wolfman marched on.

Nearer and nearer to the house of the Chief of Police.

Stomp, stomp, stomp.

The ground was shaking.

"Please, please, please go away, Wolfman,"
the Chief of Police sobbed.

But Wolfman didn't stop.

Wolfman got to the garden gate in front of the Chief of Police's house.

Wham! He kicked it over.

Up the garden path. Stomp, stomp, stomp.
Up to the door.

"Help, help, help!" the Chief of Police screamed from behind the door.

Wolfman bent down and looked through the letterbox.

The Chief of Police looked up and saw Wolfman's eyes.

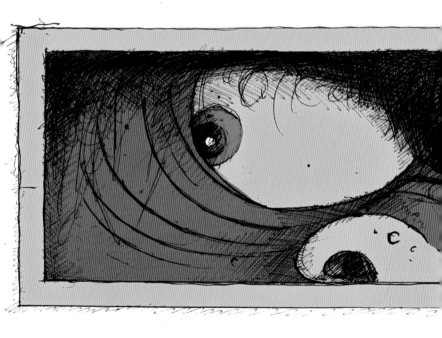

"What do you want, Wolfman?" the Chief of Police called out. "Just say! What do you want?"

There was a moment's silence.

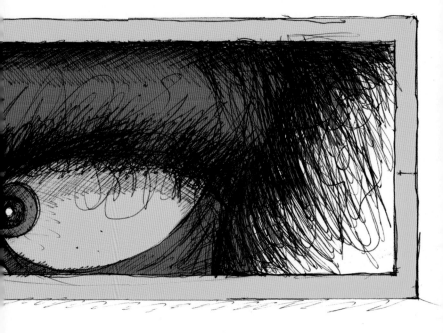

And then, in a little moany voice, Wolfman said, "Can I use your toilet?"

Are you NUTS about stories?

Read ALL the Acorns!